This **F**rog book belongs to:

....

Translated By Megan Larkin

This paperback edition first published in 2014 by Andersen Press Ltd.
20 Vauxhall Bridge Road, London SW1V 2SA.
First published in Great Britain in 1996 by Andersen Press Ltd.
Published in Australia by Random House Australia Pty.,
20 Alfred Street, Milsons Point, Sydney, NSW 2061.

Colour separated in Switzerland by Photolitho AG, Zürich.
Printed and bound in China by Foshan Zhaorong Printing Co., Ltd.

10   9   8   7   6   5   4   3   2   1

British Library Cataloguing in Publication Data available.
ISBN 978 1 78344 141 9

Frog
is Frog

Max Velthuijs

Andersen Press

"How lucky I am," said Frog, admiring his reflection in the water. "I am beautiful and I can swim and jump better than anyone. I am green, and green is my favourite colour. Being a frog is the best thing in the world."

"What about me then?" asked Duck. "I am all white.
Don't you think I am beautiful too?"
"No," said Frog. "There's no green on you at all."
"But I can fly," said Duck, "and you can't."

"Oh, yes?" said Frog. "I've never seen you fly."
"I'm a bit lazy," said Duck, "but I *can* fly. Watch."
She took a run up and flapped her wings noisily.

Then, suddenly Duck rose from the ground and flew gracefully into the air. She flew round a few times and then landed on the grass in front of Frog.

"Fantastic!" cried Frog, full of admiration. "I want to fly too."

"You can't," said Duck. "You haven't got any wings."

And she went home feeling happy.

When Frog was alone again he started to practise flying.
He took a long run up and flapped his arms wildly up
and down. But no matter how hard he tried, he couldn't
get off the ground.

Frog was disappointed.

"I am a useless frog," he thought. "I can't even fly.
If only I had wings."

Then Frog had a clever idea. Whatever Duck could do,
he could do too.

For a week Frog worked hard with an old sheet and some string. At last, he was ready for his first test flight.

He went to the hill by the river. He took a good run up, just as he had seen Duck do.

Then he leapt into the air with outstretched arms.

He hovered in the air for a few seconds, like a real bird. But then the wings ripped and he dropped like a stone. He fell in the river with a splash. At least it was a soft landing.

Rat saw Frog stumble out of the water.

"You must know that frogs cannot fly," he said.

"Can you fly?" asked Frog.

"Of course not," said Rat, "I have no wings, but I'm good at making things."

Frog thought about this on his way home. He would ask
Pig as well.

Pig was taking a cake out of the oven as Frog arrived.

"Pig, can you fly?" asked Frog.

"Certainly not," said Pig. "I would probably get airsick."

"What can you do then?" asked Frog.
"All sorts of things," replied Pig, indignantly. "I can make
the best cakes in the world. And I am beautiful. I am
pink all over, and pink is my favourite colour."
Frog had to admit that this was true.

"I bet I can make a cake too," thought Frog when he was back at home. He threw everything he could find into a bowl and began to stir, just as he had seen Pig do.

Then he threw everything into a pan and put it on the stove.

"There, you see," thought Frog. "My cake will be delicious."

But after a while, smoke began to pour from the pan and it smelt awful. The cake was completely burned.

"I can't even bake a cake," thought Frog, sadly.

He went to visit Hare.

"Hare, may I borrow a book from you?" asked Frog.

"Can you read?" asked Hare, surprised.

"No," said Frog. "Perhaps you could tell me how."

"Look," said Hare. "This is an 'o' and this is an 'a' and this is a 'k' and this..."
"Okay, I get it," said Frog, impatiently, and he ran home with the book under his arm.

He made himself comfortable and opened the book.
But the pages were full of strange scribblings.
Frog couldn't understand a word.
An hour later, he was none the wiser.
"I'll never read this!" said Frog. "It's much too
difficult for me. I'm just an ordinary, stupid frog."

Sadly, Frog returned the book to Hare.
"Well?" asked Hare. "Did you enjoy it?"
Frog shook his head sorrowfully.
"I can't read," he said. "I can't bake a cake, I can't
make things and I can't fly. You are all much cleverer
than me. I can't do anything. I'm just an ordinary
green frog," he sobbed.

"But Frog," said Hare, "I can't fly either, and I can't bake cakes or make things. I can't swim and leap like you do . . . because I am a hare. And you are a frog, and we all love you."

Deep in thought, Frog went to the river and looked at
his reflection in the water.
"That is me," he thought. "A green frog with stripy
swimming trunks."

Suddenly, Frog felt very happy.

"Hare is right," he thought. "I am lucky to be a frog."

And he leapt for joy – a big frog leap, as only frogs can do.

He felt as if he was flying.

Max Velthuijs's twelve beautiful stories about **Frog** and his friends first started to appear twenty five years ago and are now available as paperbacks, e-books and apps.

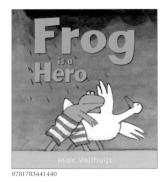
9781783441440

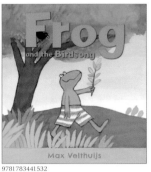
9781783441532

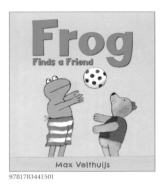
9781783441501

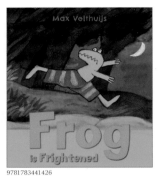
9781783441426

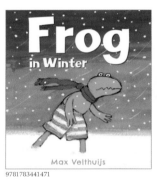
9781783441471

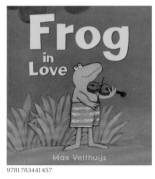
9781783441457

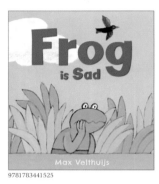
9781783441525

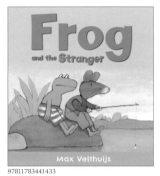
97811783441433

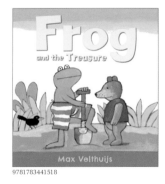
9781783441518

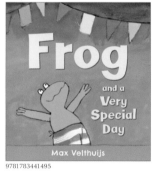
9781783441495

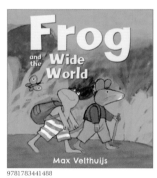
9781783441488

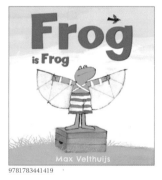
9781783441419

Max Velthuijs (Dutch for Field House) lived in the Netherlands, and received the prestigious Hans Christian Andersen Medal for Illustration. His charming stories capture childhood experiences while offering life lessons to children as young as three, and have been translated into more than forty languages.

'**Frog is an inspired creation — a masterpiece of graphic simplicity.**'
GUARDIAN

'**Miniature morality plays for our age.**' **IBBY**